Dear Parents:

Congratulations! Your child is taking the first steps on an exciting journey. The destination? Independent reading!

STEP INTO READING® will help your child get there. The program offers five steps to reading success. Each step includes fun stories and colorful art or photographs. In addition to original fiction and books with favorite characters, there are Step into Reading Non-Fiction Readers, Phonics Readers and Boxed Sets, Sticker Readers, and Comic Readers—a complete literacy program with something to interest every child.

Learning to Read, Step by Step!

Ready to Read   Preschool–Kindergarten
• big type and easy words • rhyme and rhythm • picture clues
For children who know the alphabet and are eager to begin reading.

Reading with Help   Preschool–Grade 1
• basic vocabulary • short sentences • simple stories
For children who recognize familiar words and sound out new words with help.

Reading on Your Own   Grades 1–3
• engaging characters • easy-to-follow plots • popular topics
For children who are ready to read on their own.

Reading Paragraphs   Grades 2–3
• challenging vocabulary • short paragraphs • exciting stories
For newly independent readers who read simple sentences with confidence.

Ready for Chapters   Grades 2–4
• chapters • longer paragraphs • full-color art
For children who want to take the plunge into chapter books but still like colorful pictures.

STEP INTO READING® is designed to give every child a successful reading experience. The grade levels are only guides; children will progress through the steps at their own speed, developing confidence in their reading.

Remember, a lifetime love of reading starts with a single step!

LEGO, the LEGO logo, the Brick and Knob configurations and the Minifigure
are trademarks and/or copyrights of the LEGO Group.
©2022 The LEGO Group. All rights reserved.

 Manufactured under license granted to AMEET Sp. z o.o.
by the LEGO Group.

AMEET Sp. z o.o.
Nowe Sady 6, 94–102 Łódz—Poland
ameet@ameet.eu
www.ameet.eu

www.LEGO.com

Published in the United States by Random House Children's Books, a division of Penguin Random House
LLC, 1745 Broadway, New York, NY 10019, and in Canada by Penguin Random House Canada Limited,
Toronto.

Step into Reading, Random House, and the Random House colophon are registered trademarks of
Penguin Random House LLC.

Visit us on the Web!
StepIntoReading.com
rhcbooks.com

Educators and librarians, for a variety of teaching tools, visit us at RHTeachersLibrarians.com

ISBN 978-0-593-48111-0 (trade)
ISBN 978-0-593-48112-7 (lib. bdg.)
ISBN 978-0-593-48113-4 (ebook)

Printed in the United States of America
10 9 8 7 6 5 4 3 2 1

BIRTHDAY HELPERS!

by Steve Foxe

based on the story by Stacia Deutsch

illustrated by AMEET Studio

Random House 🏠 New York

Harl Hubbs jumped out of bed.

"It is my birthday!" he shouted.

Harl loved helping

the people of LEGO® City.

To celebrate his birthday,

Harl wanted to help

as many people

as he possibly could.

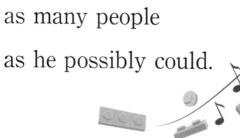

He rushed outside

to get started!

The first person Harl ran into was Lieutenant Duke DeTain. Duke was a police officer who knew a thing or two about flips and jump-kicks. "Hello, Helpful Handyman!" Duke said.

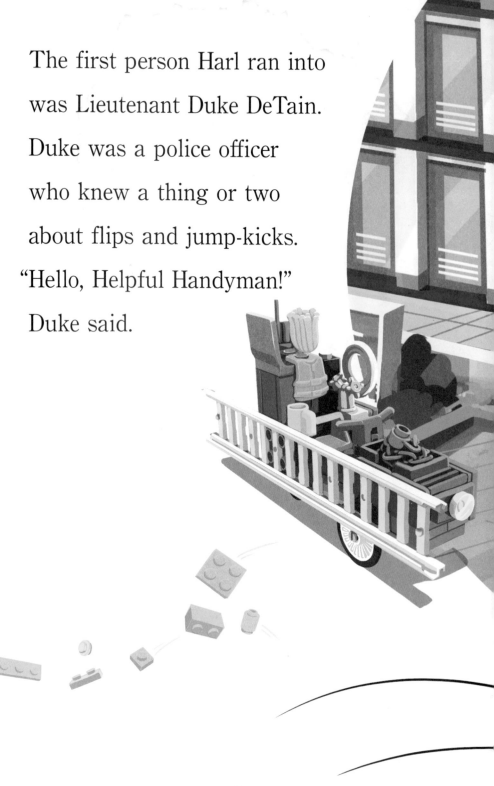

"Today is my birthday,"
said Harl.
He was planning to have
a happy, helpy day.
Harl picked up his toolbox.
"Need anything?" he asked Duke.

"No, it is a quiet day in LEGO City,"
said Duke.

"Let me know if there is
anything exciting to do."

The next person Harl saw
was Firefighter Bob.

"Need any help?" Harl asked.

"Nope," Bob replied with a yawn.

But Harl had an idea—
and a screwdriver!

Before Bob could stop him,
Harl fixed the siren
on the fire truck
to sound louder than ever.

BOCK! BOCK! BOCK!

Bob pressed the siren button.

Bock! Bock! Bock!

The siren sounded like a chicken!

Before Harl could fix it,

a fire alarm went off.

Firefighter Bob raced
to an emergency.
Harl felt bad that his help
had not gone as planned.

Down the street, Harl saw Poppy Starr.

Her stage was in pieces!

Harl got out his hammer to help.

When Poppy turned around,
the stage was fully built.
"Ta-da!" Harl said with pride.
"Thanks, Harl," Poppy replied.
"But I was taking the stage down,
not putting it up!"

Then Harl saw Shirley Keeper

carrying an empty trash can.

"I am having a rough day,"

Harl told her.

"Me too," Shirley said.

"Not much trash to collect today."

17

Harl whipped out his toolbox.

"I could upgrade your truck!"

he offered.

"No thanks," Shirley replied.

"But maybe you can join me
on my route tomorrow."
Harl frowned.
Tomorrow would not be
his special day anymore.

Duke DeTain walked by.
"Nothing exciting
is happening today,"
Harl told Duke with a big sigh.

"It is the worst birthday ever."

"But the day is not over yet!"

Duke said.

21

Harl headed home.

He was sad that he had not helped anyone.

Then someone knocked on his door.

It was Chief McCloud.

She asked Harl

to help her untangle some lights.

Next, Mayor Fleck stopped by.

"Can you pick up my groceries?"

Harl was happy to help!

Harl fixed the lights and then picked up the mayor's groceries. On his way to deliver the food, he ran into Police Chief Wheeler.

He needed Harl
to fix
the front wheel
on his skateboard.

Harl was happy to help.
Chief Wheeler gave Harl
his skateboard, and he carried
the mayor's groceries for Harl.

Harl followed Chief Wheeler

back to the police station

to get the chief's spare wheels.

When he opened the door,

he saw that all his friends were there!

"Happy birthday, Harl!"

everyone shouted.

The lights that Harl had untangled

were quickly strung up for the party.

And the groceries he had picked up

included a big birthday cake!

Firefighter Bob thanked Harl
for fixing the siren on the truck.
The clucking sounds had helped him
rescue some lost baby chicks.

Poppy Starr was grateful, too.
Her record company wanted
to hold a last-minute concert tonight,
and now her stage was all set!
Even Shirley was excited—
she would have so much trash
to pick up after Harl's party!

Duke thanked Harl for helping
so many people.
Harl was glad, but he realized he had
never found anything exciting
for Duke to do.
"Fighting crime is great,"
Duke said with a grin.
"But planning your
top-secret surprise party
was super exciting!"

Harl was so happy.

It turned out that he had

helped his friends all day long!

It was a happy, helpy day.

"This is the best birthday ever!"

Harl shouted.